For Harry and Megan. G.P.

American edition published in 2012 by Andersen Press USA, an imprint of Andersen Press Ltd. www.andersenpressusa.com
First published in Great Britain in 2012 by Andersen Press Ltd., 20 Vauxhall Bridge Road, London SW1V 2SA.
Published in Australia by Random House Australia Pty., Level 3, 100 Pacific Highway, North Sydney, NSW 2060.
Text copyright © Gervase Phinn, 2012. Illustration copyright © Tony Ross, 2012.
Distributed in the United States and Canada by Lerner Publishing Group, Inc.
241 First Avenue North Minneapolis, MN 55401 U.S.A. www.lernerbooks.com

Color separated in Switzerland by Photolitho AG, Zürich. Printed and bound in Singapore by Tien Wah Press.
Tony Ross has used pen, ink, and watercolor in this book.

Library of Congress Cataloging-in-Publication Data Available. ISBN: 978-0-7613-8996-5
1 – TWP – 12/31/11
This book has been printed on acid-free paper.

Who Am I?

GERVASE PHINN   TONY ROSS

Andersen Press USA

One hot, hot day in the middle of the deep, deep jungle, a strange little creature hatched out of an egg.

He **scratched** ...

and he **yawned** ...

and he **opened**
his **big** round
eyes and looked
around him.

"Who am I?" he asked himself. "Where do I come from?"
Off he went plodding through the tall, tall grass to find out.

Soon he met a creature with a **very long** neck.

"Excuse me," said the strange little creature chirpily. "Could you tell me **who I am** and **where I come from?**"

"**I have no idea,**" chuckled the creature. "I know that I am the **giraffe** and I am the **tallest** animal in the whole **wide world**, but I do not know what sort of creature you are."

So the strange little creature plodded on through the tall grass.

Soon he met a creature with a long nose.

"Excuse me," said the strange little creature cheerfully. "Could you tell me who I am and where I come from?"

"I have no idea," trumpeted the creature. "I know that I am the elephant and I am the strongest animal in the whole wide world, but I do not know what sort of creature you are."

So the strange little creature plodded on through the tall grass.

Soon he met a creature with very long legs.

"Excuse me," said the strange little creature shyly.
"Could you tell me who I am and where I come from?"

"I have no idea," snarled the creature. "I know that
I am the cheetah and I am the fastest animal in the
whole wide world, but I do not know what sort of
creature you are."

So the strange little creature plodded on through the
tall grass.

Soon he met a creature with a **sharp, pointed** horn.

"Excuse me," said the strange little creature anxiously.
"Could you tell me **who I am** and **where I come from?**"

"**I have no idea,**" snorted the creature. "I know that
I am the rhinoceros and I am the **toughest** animal in
the whole **wide world**, but I do not know what sort of
creature you are."

So the strange little creature plodded on through the tall
grass.

Soon he met a creature with a very hairy body.

"Excuse me," said the strange little creature timidly.
"Could you tell me who I am and where I come from?"

"I have no idea," chattered the creature. "I know that I am
the chimpanzee and I am the cleverest animal in the
whole wide world, but I do not know what sort of
creature you are."

So the strange little creature
plodded on through
the tall grass.

Soon he came to a deep, dark, muddy river, and there, resting on the bank, was a creature with great yellow eyes and a wide smiling mouth.

"Excuse me," said the strange little creature desperately. "Could you tell me who I am and where I come from?"

"Yes I can," snapped the creature.

"You can!" exclaimed the strange little creature.

"I can, but you will have to come a little closer," whispered the creature, smiling and opening wide his jaws.

"Climb on my nose and I will tell you."

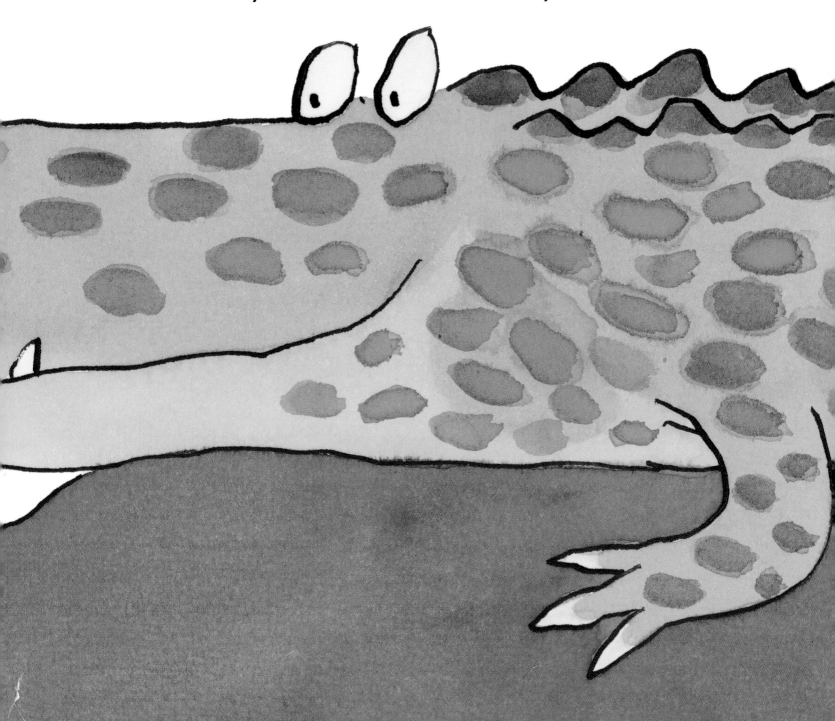

So the strange little creature plodded **closer**...

and **closer**...

and **closer**...

and just as he was about to climb
onto the **crocodile's** nose . . .

he heard a voice behind him.

"There you are!"

He turned to see a creature just like him but
much, much bigger.

"Who are you?"
asked the strange little creature.

"I'm your mother," said the big strange creature,
"and you're my little baby chameleon,
the most beautiful and unusual creature in
the whole wide world!
I have been wandering around the jungle,
wondering where you were.

Now, come along and meet
your brothers and sisters."